D1096986

Yogi Bear Saves Jellystone Park

Story by Horace J. Elias

Distributed by MODERN PROMOTIONS
A Division of UNISYSTEMS, INC., NEW YORK, N.Y.
Published by Ottenheimer Publishers, Inc.

Jellystone Park was a wonderful place to grow up and live in, particularly if you happened to be a mischievous, fun-loving, young bear named Yogi. The only trouble with Jellystone was that, in spite of the fact that

3

it was over three thousand square miles in size, it wasn't quite big enough for both Ranger Smith and Yogi Bear!

Ranger Smith liked Yogi — he really did, in spite of the fact that Yogi was a constant problem. By the same token, Yogi liked the Ranger, even though the Ranger had punished him many, many times for the trouble Yogi was forever getting himself into with his antics.

One summer, however, things got completely out of hand. It began like this: for three nights in a row, the Ranger baked a pie for himself and placed it on the window ledge to cool overnight. Yogi came by on each of those three nights and swiped the pies!

On the morning after the night Yogi swiped the third pie, Ranger Smith stood outside of his cabin, looking at the land which sloped gently

up into the surrounding hills. "I know you're up there somewhere, Yogi," he said to himself. "And you're probably watching my cabin right now. Maybe tonight we can do something to make you not quite so happy about swiping those pies!"

Yogi wasn't watching the cabin, as it happened. With Boo Boo, his very young bear friend, he was lying on his back under a tree in a meadow, smiling up at the

blue sky.

"Boo Boo," said Yogi, "I think this is the best summer yet. Plenty to eat, the weather's perfect, and those *pies*! Oh, my—I never tasted anything so good!" Then he rolled over and looked at Boo Boo. "I wonder what kind he'll bake tonight?" he went on.

"Don't you think maybe three nights in a row is enough, Yogi?" said Boo Boo, who was getting a little nerv-

ous about the whole thing. "Suppose he's waiting for you tonight and catches you at it?"

"Never happen!" laughed Yogi. "He's got to go to sleep sometime. As long as he wants to bake 'em and put 'em on that ledge overnight to cool, I'll get 'em, and *we'll* eat 'em!"

That night, Yogi crept down to a spot near the Ranger's cabin and waited until he was sure the Ranger

was asleep. Then he tiptoed the short distance to the kitchen window, and there it was! Another pie on the ledge was cooling in the night air!

Yogi scooped it up and looked at it in the moonlight. "Hey! How about that!" he thought. "Lemon meringue!" And he hurried on back to the cave house he shared with Boo Boo and went to sleep.

In the morning, he shook Boo Boo awake. "Huh?" said

Boo Boo. "What's wrong, Yogi?"

"Not a thing!" cried Yogi. "It's another beautiful summer day, and we have an extra special treat for breakfast. It's lemon meringue pie, baked with loving care by our friend Ranger Smith. Only *we're* gonna eat it, not him!"

"I don't know about this," said Boo Boo. "I never had lemon meringue pie for breakfast before!"

"Well, you're gonna have it this morning!" laughed Yogi. "Here's your slice. Excuse me if I don't wait. I know my manners are bad, but my appetite's worse!" And he took a huge bite of the pie.

For a few seconds nothing happened, as Yogi started to chew. Then he got a strange look on his face, groaned something that sounded like, "Gug-gug-gug *aaarrghh!*" and ran out of the cave. Boo Boo just sat there, staring at

the piece of pie he was holding and looking from it to the door and back again.

After a few minutes, Yogi came staggering weakly back into the cave house. It's very difficult for a bear to look pale, because of all the hair. Perhaps it would be best to say that if a bear *can* look pale, Yogi did, *underneath* the hair!

"Whoosh!" he said, as he collapsed into a corner.

"What happened?" said Boo Boo.

"Take your little finger and stick it into the meringue, then taste it," said Yogi.

Boo Boo looked at Yogi, then stuck his finger into the white meringue and put the finger into his mouth. Then he made a terrible face and said "*Yick!*"

"The meringue," said Yogi, "is whipped soap. Now do the same with the filling."

Boo Boo put the tip of a finger into the filling. "My

gosh!" he said. "It doesn't even *feel* like the lemon-y stuff that's supposed to be there. It feels kinda *slippery!*"

"It feels slippery because it *is* slippery!" said Yogi. "The inside of the pie is made of vaseline!"

"The big bite you took," asked Boo Boo. "Did you—?"

"Enough," answered Yogi, with a weak smile. "Why do you think I ran out of here?"

"Oof!" said Boo Boo. "Lemon meringue pie made of

whipped soap and vaseline! I guess you better stay away from the cabin for a while, Yogi!"

"Hmmmm," said Yogi. "Let's just think about that for a little bit. The Ranger is gonna figure he got even with that doctored lemon meringue pie. And I have to admit he fooled me pretty good! But now, he's gonna think I've learned my lesson. He's sure I won't dare go near his cabin, for fear this

time he'll either be waitin
for me, or it'll be anothe
awful kind of pie."

"So?" asked Boo Boo.

"So he's gonna be sure I'n
not coming back," went o
Yogi. "And he'll bak
another one tonight. Bu
this'll be a *good* one—only
I'm gonna fool *him* and swip
it!"

Ranger Smith, however
had other ideas. He knew
Yogi better than Yogi knew
himself, and what he did wa

bake another pie and leave it
outside to cool. And that
night, he stayed awake to
watch, hiding in some bushes
a short distance from the
cabin.

Sure enough, around mid-
night, the Ranger saw Yogi
approaching the cabin. He
saw the bear sniff at the
aroma from the pie. Then
Yogi dashed to the window,
grabbed the pie, and as he
bustled away, the Ranger
heard him whisper, "Oh, boy!

Smell those apples! Delicious!"

And then, just as Ranger Smith had hoped, Yogi couldn't stand it any longer. He stopped and took a big bite of the pie!

Five seconds later, the Ranger heard something he'd never heard before—a bear screaming! Yogi had bitten right through the pie, which consisted of a top layer of apples, with nothing but pepper underneath. Then he heard

Yogi bellow, "Water! Water!" and finally, a big splash, as Yogi jumped into the lake to cool off his burning mouth.

Next morning Boo Boo said to Yogi, "What was all the racket at the cabin last night? I heard a lot of noise, but you didn't come back for so long, I fell asleep!"

"He did it again," answered Yogi. "He baked another pie to trick me! This one was full of pepper!" He paused for a moment, then

said, "I won't be around much today, Boo Boo. I'm going off by myself to think. He's not gonna get away with this. I'm gonna figure out a way to get even!" And he marched out of the cave. Late in the afternoon, he returned.

"Boo Boo," he said, "let's go to sleep right now."

"But, Yogi," said Boo Boo. "It's still daytime! It's too early to go to sleep!"

"We're going to sleep now, because we'll be up most of

the night," answered Yogi. "I'm gonna set the alarm for midnight, which is when we get up and go to work!"

When the alarm woke Yogi and Boo Boo at midnight, Yogi said, "You get everything ready to bake a pie, Boo Boo. I'll be back in a little while!"

"Hey! What's going on, Yogi?" asked the little bear. "You going someplace?"

"Going to the Ranger's cabin to check something

out," replied Yogi. "If I find what I expect to find, we'll get even tomorrow!"

In a little over an hour, Yogi returned carrying a pie. "Let's see what's in this one," he said. Then he poked into the pie, brought out a small piece of the filling and sniffed it cautiously. "Hmmmm," he said. "This is what I was hoping for! It's pumpkin pie with powdered sugar on top!"

"Are we going to eat it now?" asked Boo Boo.

"No, I think we'll wait," replied Yogi. "Right now we're gonna bake a pie that looks exactly like this one. It's gonna taste a little different, though, because the filling is gonna be mashed onions, turnips and a *lot* of vinegar. Then we put the sugar on top, and we'll find out how much *he* likes it!"

A couple of hours later, the onion, turnip and vinegar pie was ready. Yogi made his way to the Ranger's cabin

and placed it on the window ledge, exactly where the pumpkin pie had been. Then he returned to the cave, and he and Boo Boo went to sleep.

Unfortunately for Yogi's plans, however, the Ranger had a plan of his own. He was awake and saw Yogi swipe the pumpkin pie. He was still awake when Yogi returned with the onion pie. The Ranger tested the onion pie and thought for a few minutes. Then, an hour later,

he climbed to Yogi's cave. He made sure Yogi and Boo Boo were asleep, then crept noiselessly into the cave and exchanged the two pies!

It was when Yogi took the first bite of the onion pie and realized he'd been tricked again, that he lost his temper completely and went out of control!

For the next week, the Ranger's office was swamped with complaints from all kinds of people.

Furious campers complained that their food was being stolen, but not even eaten. It was just being strewn around.

Motorists complained about having to leave their cars to clear away piles of rocks, trees and underbrush they found blocking the Jellystone roads.

Other campers came growling that some of their canoes had been cut loose and left to drift for miles downstream.

Still others yelled about canoes being filled with stones to sink them where they were tied up.

The last straw, however, was the beavers! It seemed as though every beaver dam in the park had been pulled apart, and the quiet little ponds were gone, leaving the beavers homeless.

The morning after Ranger Smith got the news about the beaver dams, he called in the other rangers for a meeting.

"Men," he said, "I think you all know how I feel about Yogi Bear. I like him, in spite of the fact that he's mischievous and too full of high spirits for his own good. But now he's gone too far. Once before, he pulled that trick of tearing down the beaver dams. If you remember, we almost had a beaver revolution on our hands. They threatened at that time to build one monster dam which would make a

lake out of the entire park, unless Yogi repaired their little dams. This time we're going to have to do it ourselves, and it'll take weeks."

"What about Yogi, Ranger Smith?" asked one of the Rangers.

"As I said, this time he's gone too far!" was the reply. "I've been on the phone with Superintendent Simpson and Commissioner Phudd, and they agree. Yogi and Boo Boo have got to go—for good! And

if he won't agree to that, they'll be captured and sent to a zoo! Now let's get to work on those beaver dams, and wherever you go in the park, you leave that message for Yogi!" Then he paused for a moment and said, "On second thought, change that message. Instead, leave this word with everyone you see...Tell Yogi I want to see him and Boo Boo — and in the biggest kind of a hurry!"

By the time Yogi got the

message late the next day, he was over his terrible temper tantrum. He was beginning to worry about what was going to happen to him because of the damage he had done during his outburst.

"Well," he said to Boo Boo, "I guess whatever it is, I've got it coming to me!"

"You had this whole park in a pretty good mess for a while!" agreed Boo Boo.

"C'mon, chum," said Yogi. "Let's go get it over with!"

When the two bears entered the Ranger's cabin a little while later, he looked at them for a moment and then said, "Sit down. I have something to say to you two."

Yogi said, "Ranger Smith, none of this was Boo Boo's fault, so if anybody's gonna be punished, it should be me!"

The Ranger said, "Maybe he didn't start it, but he was sure enough along for the ride. Do you know the thing

that makes me feel bad about this? It's you, Yogi. You can dish it out, but you can't take it! You began this business by swiping my pies. Then when I decided to teach you a lesson by doctoring up a couple, you had to figure out a way to get even. When that backfired on you, you blew up! And now, you're in the worst trouble you've ever been in in your life!"

"OK, Ranger Smith," said Yogi quietly. "Tell us what

we have to do to make up for whatever we did. Maybe I can stop blowing up from now on!"

"It won't make any difference," said the Ranger, "because you won't be here—in Jellystone Park, that is."

"I don't know what you mean," said Yogi. "Where are we going?"

"That's entirely up to you," answered Ranger Smith. "But you're leaving Jellystone for good! If you won't go,

I have orders to cage you and ship you off to a zoo!"

Yogi just looked at the Ranger for a moment or two! Then he looked at Boo Boo and grinned. "Hey, Boo Boo!" he said, "I think they're mad at us around here!" Then he turned to the Ranger and said, "How about if I repair all the beaver dams and get back all the canoes and generally straighten out everything? Then, we'll—"

The Ranger interrupted.

"No, Yogi," he said. "In the first place, the campers are so mad, that if they caught you messing around with canoes, they'd be liable to shoot you on sight. In the second place—you are going *out* of Jellystone Park—for all time! You can have twenty-four hours to get ready. After that time, if you're seen in the Park, we have orders to run you down and cage you and Boo Boo!"

Yogi stared at the floor,

then he finally looked up and walked to the door. "Let's go, Boo Boo," he said. Then he said, "Good-bye, Ranger Smith."

"G'by, Ranger," said Boo Boo, and they left.

As they trudged away, Boo Boo said, "You think he meant it, Yogi?"

"He meant it, all right," answered Yogi. "Let's get up to the cave. We've got some hard thinking to do!"

When they arrived at the

cave, Yogi stretched out on his bed and closed his eyes. Boo Boo said, "You going to sleep, Yogi?"

Yogi, without opening his eyes, said, "I'm thinking, Boo Boo. Why don't you stretch out and take a little nap?"

"Heck, Yogi, I can't sleep!" cried Boo Boo. "I'm scared! Gee whiz—where can we go? We've never *lived* anyplace but right here in Jellystone!"

"I don't know yet," answered Yogi. "That's why I

want to just lay here an
think." Then he sat up an
said, "But I can tell you on
thing for sure, chum. *We ar
not leaving Jellystone Park!*"

"But how can we stay
Yogi?" wailed Boo Boo. "If w
stay, somebody's sure to se
us *some*time, and I don'
want to spend the rest of m
life walking up and dow
inside a cage in a zoo!"

"Neither do I!" answere
Yogi. "And that's why I kee
telling you I've got to think

Now if you can't sleep, at least stop asking questions so I can concentrate!"

"OK, Yogi," answered Boo Boo. "I'm going outside and sit in the sun. It may be the last chance I get to do it in the park!"

Late in the afternoon, Boo Boo went back into the cave. Yogi was still stretched out on the bed, but he was fast asleep and snoring!

"What th-?" said Boo Boo aloud. "He's supposed to be

thinking! Hey, Yogi! Wake up!"

Yogi stirred, yawned and opened one eye. "Hello, there, Boo Boo," he said. "How was it in the sun?"

"Yogi!" cried Boo Boo. "Here we are thrown out of Jellystone Park, and you're sound asleep instead of figuring something out for us!"

"Oh," replied Yogi. "That. All taken care of, chum. We go right after dinner."

"Go? Go where??" asked

the bewildered Boo Boo. "What did you figure out?"

"Well, I'll tell you," explained Yogi. "I spent quite a lot of time trying to think up something, or some way, to get the Ranger to forgive us and let us stay. But no matter what I thought of, I just couldn't get over one thing. This time he *means* it, and aside from that, he's got orders from Superintendent Simpson and Commissioner Phudd. So, we're going."

"But you haven't answered my question, Yogi," cried Boo Boo. "Going where? You said we weren't going to leave the Park, no matter *what* the Ranger said. So how can we stay?"

"Easy," answered Yogi. We go someplace they'll never find us! Then we stay there for a while, and one day when this whole thing has been forgotten, we come home!"

"I'm not very old or very

smart, I guess," said Boo Boo. "But where can we go where nobody will ever find us? Is there a place like that in the park?"

"Do you know how big Jellystone Park is?" said Yogi. "It's so big there are parts of it where no one has ever been! There's one spot in particular that we can go to—and they not only won't *find* us—they wouldn't even dream of *looking* for us there!"

"Where's that, Yogi? Is it a long way from here?"

"I figure on about four days travel," answered Yogi.

"You haven't said *where*!" insisted Boo Boo.

"Lake Miserable, up in the Awful Mountains," replied Yogi.

"Lake What in the *Which* Mountains?" yelled the little bear. "I never even heard of such a place! It sounds terrible! Couldn't we go someplace with a better name?"

"That name is our best protection!" said Yogi. "The Ranger told me once that some people went up there camping one time and came back talking about that miserable lake and those awful mountains. That's how they came to call them by those names! They claimed the country up there was so wild, they hated it! And besides, they said there was thunder up there all day long, even when the sun was out and

there wasn't a cloud in the sky!"

"Doesn't sound like much of a place for us to live, does it, though?" said Boo Boo. "And if it's so wild, there are probably animals! Bears and stuff!"

Yogi laughed. "I don't know whether you've looked in the mirror lately chum—but you happen to *be* a bear—and me, too!"

Boo Boo thought for a moment. Then he smiled and

said, "Well, I'll be swizzled! How'd I happen to forget *that*?"

"I guess we've been hanging around with the Ranger too long," answered Yogi. "We're going back to being bears who live in the wild woods!" Then he chuckled a couple of times and said, "Maybe you better start practicing making dangerous-looking faces, Boo Boo! We might have to scare off a few rabbits or squirrels!"

"OK," said Boo Boo. "Count me in. When do we go? Tommorrow morning?"

"Nope," answered Yogi. "Late tonight. We have dinner, take a nap and leave around midnight. If that Ranger's baked another pie, I'd like to take it along for a souvenir!"

Late that night, Yogi and Boo Boo took a last look around the cave, closed it up and left. When they arrived at the Ranger's cabin, sure

enough, there was a pie cooling on the window ledge! Yogi crept to the window and returned with a funny look on his face.

"What's the matter, Yogi? Did the Ranger put out another uggy pie?" asked the little bear.

"No, I don't think so," answered Yogi. "Look at this." He handed Boo Boo a note "Oh. I forgot—you can't read yet. The note says 'Good-bye, good luck and enjoy the pie.

But don't come back!' "

"Looks as though he figured us out pretty good, huh?" said Boo Boo.

"Well," said Yogi, "at least we've got one pie more than we thought we had! Let's go!"

"Lake Miserable in the Awful Mountains, here we come!" cried Boo Boo, and the two bears set out on what was supposed to be their farewell trip out of Jellystone Park.

Yogi's idea about how long

it would take them to get to where they were going wasn't very accurate. It was almost two weeks later that they came out of a big patch of woods and saw a small lake nestled in the side of the mountain they'd been climbing. All around them, jagged, nasty-looking mountain peaks poked into the sky. The lake seemed to be in constant motion. One minute there were small waves, then

big waves would dash against the rocky shore.

Yogi took a slow look around. "Well, Boo Boo," he said, "I can see why they call them the Awful Mountains! They sure don't look very friendly!"

"How about the lake?" said Boo Boo. "I never saw waves like that on a lake, except if there was a lot of wind and a storm!"

"I know one reason those people didn't like it up here,"

laughed Yogi. "Those woods are full of poison ivy. *What's that*!??" he cried, as a tremendous, rolling, thunderous noise echoed through the mountainside.

"I guess that's what those people were talking about when they said it thundered all day, even with a clear sky and sunshine!" answered Boo Boo.

"It's a funny kind of noise, though," said Yogi. "It

sounds *almost* like thunder, but not really!"

"Could it be the mountains, sort of settling down or something?" Boo Boo said.

"I just don't know," replied Yogi. "I guess we'll get used to it. We'd better—because this is home—at least for while! Let's find us a good place to sleep, and tomorrow we'll look around."

A little scouting turned up a good-sized cave, dry and comfortable. The two bears

got themselves settled, and just before they went to sleep, Yogi sat up and said, "Notice anything, Boo Boo?"

Boo Boo thought for a bit and said, "Can't think of anything, Yogi. What is it?"

"A little while after it got dark," Yogi explained, "that noise stopped!"

Boo Boo listened for a moment. Then he said, "Maybe the mountains got tired and went to sleep!"

"Maybe that's what we

should do, too!" laughed Yogi. "I know *I'm* tired. That was a tough climb today. Tomorrow's another day, and then we take a good look and see what kind of company we have! Good night, Boo Boo!"

Next morning, Yogi and Boo Boo were up and around at daybreak. They walked down to the edge of the lake just as the sun peeked over the horizon. "Boo Boo! Look at how calm the lake is! And that thundering noise hasn't

started up again!" cried Yogi.

"If the people who visited here before had seen it like this, they'd have called it Lake Peaceful or something!" said Boo Boo. "It looks real pretty now!"

Just as Boo Boo finished speaking, there was a tremendous roll of the thundering noise. A few seconds later, the water in the lake began to churn into waves, just as they had seen it when they arrived the day before.

"What th-?" said Yogi. "First the noise, then the lake gets full of waves! I never heard of noise being able to make waves!"

"Maybe it *is* the mountains settling down!" said Boo Boo.

"Can't be," said Yogi "Why would it stop at night?"

"Well," said the little bear, "we're not going to find anything out standing here. How about it? Can we take a walk and see what's going on in our new home?"

"Good idea!" said Yogi. "Let's go. Maybe we can find ourselves a little breakfast on the way!"

Off they went exploring. They found wild berries right near the lake and managed to eat quite a lot of them. Bees were everywhere. They found a hive full of honey and put most of that on top of the berries. A little later in the morning, they were crossing another meadow, when Yogi tripped over a low bush

and fell. Immediately they heard a thin, screeching noise that sounded as though it were making words. But the noise was so shrill, they couldn't really tell. Perhaps the best way to describe the noise is this: if a small, tin whistle (the kind you used to get as a prize in a box of candy or candy popcorn) could talk, that's how it would sound.

What th-?" said Yogi, for the second time that morn-

ing, as he scrambled to his feet.

"Hey!" cried Boo Boo. "Cut that out!"

"Cut what out?" said Yogi.

"Not you!" said Boo Boo. "Something's kicking me in the ankle!" And all the while the shrill, screeching nois continued. "And whatever' making that noise is giving me a headache!" he continued.

"Well, now, just one dog goned minute!" said Yogi,

"This place is crazy! First we have thundery noises that make waves. Now we have high, squeally noises that kick people! Boo Boo, we have a mystery on our— LOOK OUT!" Just as he yelled, he made a dive at the bush he had tripped over. Boo Boo barely had time to scramble out of the way as Yogi made his dive. When Yogi got to his feet, he had something small and green squirming in his big paw.

"What's *that*?" exclaimed Boo Boo.

"*That*," said Yogi, "is what was giving you the headache and kicking you!" He looked at what was clutched in his paw more closely. Then he said, "I do *not* believe it. It can't be!"

"What? What's going on?? What *is* that thing???" yelled a completely confused Boo Boo.

"First of all, I don't think it's a thing! I think it's a *per-*

son!" said Yogi. "And I also think that *whatever* it is, it's trying to tell us something!" He looked closely once more at his paw and then listened to the noise again. Then he said to whatever was wriggling in his paw, "Could you please stop yelling and speak more slowly? Maybe then we could understand you!"

This brought another outburst of screeching. Yogi looked puzzled, then said to Boo Boo, "I think he wants

me to put him down, but if I do, I'm afraid he'll scoot away!" He squatted down and said to the green wriggler, "I'll put you down, but we want to talk to you. Will you stay?"

More noise, but quieter this time. Boo Boo thought he heard "Yes! Yes! But get out of my valley first!"

Boo Boo looked around. "What valley?" he said to Yogi. "Do you see a valley anywhere?"

"I guess if he says it's a valley, it's a valley!" said Yogi. "It just looks like a wrinkle in the meadow to me! Tell you what," he went on. "Step over here a few feet and I'll put him down. Maybe that'll stop the noise!"

Yogi and Boo Boo moved away about ten feet, and then Yogi placed whatever it was very carefully on the ground. Boo Boo and Yogi both sat down to get a better look.

Facing them was a tiny man. He was bright green, and he was furious!

"Golly!" exclaimed Boo Boo. "He's so *little*! And so green!"

This brought another screeching outburst from the tiny green man. Both bears heard a few words like "big clumsy clods" and "stupid idiot" and something about "trampled my corn crop!"

"Corn crop! What corn crop? Yogi, did we see any

corn growing over there?" said Boo Boo.

"Hold it a minute," said Yogi. He got up and started for the spot where they had been standing when Boo Boo got kicked in the ankle.

The screeching started up again immediately. This time Boo Boo heard it clearly. "No! No!! *Not again!* Look out *for my peas and tomatoes!*"

"Yogi!" yelled Boo Boo. "Hold it! Don't move!"

Yogi stopped with one foot

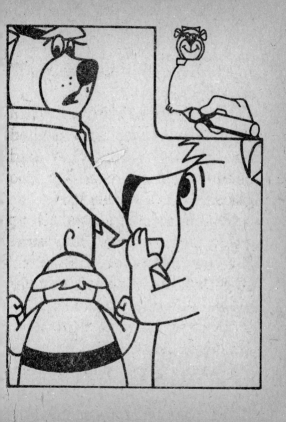

in the air. "What's wrong?" he said.

"There's peas and tomatoes over there, too!" cried Boo Boo.

"Holy smoke!" said Yogi. "What's he got, an invisible vegetable farm?"

"Come on back, Yogi," said Boo Boo. "Maybe we'd better talk to this little green guy before we do anything else!"

"OK," said Yogi. He came back and sat down. Finally Yogi said, "My name's Yogi

Bear. This young fellow is my friend Boo Boo. Who are you?"

The tiny green man looked suspiciously from Yogi to Boo Boo and back again. Then he frowned a tiny frown and said in his tiny voice, "I am the Jolly Green Midget! My name is Oliver Irk. What are you doing in my valley, besides knocking down my corn?"

"We were just out for a walk, taking a look around,"

answered Boo Boo.

"That's the trouble with you bears! You just stumble around, never look where you're going, and knock down anything that gets in your way!" snapped the green man.

"We didn't know anything *was* in our way!" said Yogi. "We're sorry if we didn't see your corn, but it's so small, it just looks like a little different kind of grass!"

"Sorry, won't help one lit-

tle bit! If you'd look where you're going, maybe you wouldn't be so blasted clumsy!" Oliver Irk said, getting madder and madder.

"Heck, if it's all that important, why didn't you put up a sign?" said Yogi. Before the Jolly Green Midget could reply, Yogi said, "I guess not. It would be so small, we couldn't read it!"

Boo Boo spoke up. "Yogi, that name sure doesn't go with his disposition!"

"You sure said a mouthful," said Yogi. "He should be called the *Grouchy* Green Midget!" Then he said, "Just how tall are you? And how big is your valley?"

"It's none of your business, really," was the reply, "but if I don't tell you what you want to know, you'll just stumble around and do some more damage!" He drew himself erect. "I am exactly thirty-three point-three millimeters tall!"

"That's a big help!" said Yogi. "How much is that in inches?"

"Just as I thought!" squealed the Jolly Green Midget. "You're ignorant, as well as stupid! Anyone knows that thirty-three point-three millimeters is exactly thirteen inches!"

"See that, Boo Boo? said Yogi. "You learn something new every day! Maybe if we stay here long enough, we

could get a college education!"

"Thirteen inches — that isn't very much, is it?" said Boo Boo, more to himself than to anyone else. "I wonder how big that valley is?"

"Since you'd just look even more stupid if I told you in millimeters, I'll have to tell you in feet! My valley is eleven feet wide and nine feet long," answered Oliver Irk.

"If we're very careful, can we look at it?" asked Yogi.

"I'd like to see what's growing in there!"

Oliver considered this for a moment and then said, "Since there's no way I can stop you, I suppose it's all right. But don't step on anything!"

Yogi and Boo Boo walked the few feet to the edge of what Yogi had called 'a wrinkle in the meadow.' Then they laid down and looked. "I see the corn, now," said Boo Boo. "The stalks are

just about the same size as Oliver!"

Yogi moved his head closer. "I see an ear on one of the stalks!" he cried. "My goodness, Boo Boo, it's only about an inch long! Golly, the kernels must be the size of beads!"

"They're just right for my teeth!" said Oliver, who was standing right next to Yogi's head. "I grow things for *me*, not you big, clumsy, overgrown animals!"

"Is that red thing a tomato?" piped up Boo Boo. "It's only about half as big as a grape!"

"I can't even *see* the peas!" said Yogi. "They must be smaller than the kernels of corn!"

"Haven't you seen enough?" said Oliver Irk. "Let's get away from here before one of you sneezes and blows down my whole farm!"

Yogi and Boo Boo got carefully to their feet and moved

away from Oliver's farm. Then they sat down in the grass and waited for the green midget to catch up to them.

"Oliver," said Yogi, "can I ask you a few questions? There are some things going on around here we don't understand, and maybe you know some of the answers!"

Oliver took a few seconds to catch his breath. He had been running hard, trying to keep up with Yogi and Boo

Boo. Finally he said, "No guarantees! But if you two promise to keep away from my valley, maybe I'll answer the questions. And then again, maybe I won't!"

Boo Boo blurted, "Well, first of all, why are you so doggone *mad* all the time?"

This provoked Oliver so much more that his voice got very high and thin. He talked so fast, Yogi and Boo Boo couldn't understand one single word. Yogi waited

until the little green man stopped and said, "Oliver, could you please not get so excited? We can't even *guess* what you just said!"

Oliver took several deep breaths, getting himself under control. Then he began, more slowly this time. "I'll tell you why I'm mad all the time! How would you like it if practically everything was bigger than you? Even squirrels and rabbits! Some of those big jack rabbits

around here look as big to me
as a horse does to a person
And they come into my valley and try to eat everything
I grow! How would you like it
if you had a farm and
elephants wanted to eat everything up?" He stopped for
some more deep breaths and
then began again. "But that's
not the worst. I'm lonesome!
There's nobody to talk to!
Day and night, night and
day, I fight squirrels and
rabbits! I'm getting so sick of

the whole thing that I'd leave, if I knew of someplace to go!"

"How long have you been here?" asked Yogi.

"I have no idea," answered Oliver. "Maybe forever, for all I know. It's been a long, long time. For instance, I can remember when those mountains didn't look at all the way they do now. A lot of them used to throw out smoke!"

Then Boo Boo asked another

unfortunate question. "How'd you happen to get so *green*?"

This set Oliver off again. "How do *I* know how I got green?" he screeched. "I'm *green*, that's all! I certainly don't know what *you're* so proud of! That moth-eaten fur rug you're wearing isn't the best-looking thing I've ever seen! And as for that Ranger—he looks like a ghost!"

"Ranger? You mean Ranger Smith?" said Yogi.

"You know him?"

"I don't know his name, but I've seen him lots of times," snapped Oliver. "Stood right next to him once. He probably thought I was a big head of lettuce or a watermelon or something! He never notices *anything*!"

Yogi smiled sadly. "Except when we steal pies," he said.

"I don't know what you're talking about," said Oliver.

"Never mind," said Yogi. "Maybe you can answer this,

170

though. Why does the water
in the lake jump around so? I
never saw waves like that in
any other lake. And what
makes that noise like thunder, when there's not a cloud
in the sky?"

Oliver didn't answer.
Instead, he snatched up a
small piece of tree branch
and scurried toward his valley. Yogi and Boo Boo heard
some screeches and squeals
and chattering. They jumped
to their feet and hurried the

few paces to where the noise was coming from. On the edge of the 'farm', Oliver was trying to beat off two rabbits and a squirrel. He was fighting a losing battle, though, because while he was driving off one, the other two kept moving in on the vegetables!

The entire situation changed immediately when Yogi and Boo Boo arrived. The squirrel and the two rabbits took one look at the

two bears and raced away in fear of their lives!

Oliver, breathing hard again, looked around. "Oh," he said, when he squinted up and saw Yogi and Boo Boo. "I was wondering why they took off like that! You know what? Maybe you're good for something, after all! How'd you two like to be tomato-, corn-, and pea-sitters?"

"Well," said Yogi, "I don't know about *that*! Let's go back and sit down again."

When they were all seated, Boo Boo said, "Please don't get mad at this, Oliver. I just thought maybe I could get a flat piece of wood and squeeze some blackberry juice. Then Yogi could make some signs!"

"Like what, for instance?" asked Oliver.

"Well, one of them could say *This is the valley of the Jolly Green Midget. Keep out!*" answered Boo Boo.

"You know," said Oliver to

Yogi, "I think you two mean well. I really do. But would you do something? Just explain clearly to your young friend here that rabbits and squirrels can't read signs or anything *else,* for that matter!"

"Don't get all upset about it," answered Yogi. "He's still pretty young and has a lot to learn. Now just before you declared war on the squirrel and those rabbits, I asked a

question. Do you know the answer?"

"The war, as you put it," said Oliver, "drove it right out of my head. What did you ask?"

"The waves in the lake," said Yogi. "And the noise that-" He stopped and listened. "There it is again! What's making that noise?"

"Oh, *that* noise!" said Oliver. "Sleepyhead!"

"Sleepyhead? What's that?" asked Yogi.

"Notice that's the first time you've heard it today?" Oliver said.

"Come to think of it, I believe you're right!" said Yogi. "What's Sleepyhead? One of the mountains around here?"

"Not quite, but you're close!" answered Oliver. "It's my brother," he went on. "He's a disgrace! The sun's been up for over an hour, and he's just getting himself awake and moving!"

All three listened as the

noise rolled again, echoing through the mountains. "You have a *brother,* and *he's* making that noise?" asked Yogi.

Boo Boo said, "I'm afraid you may get mad at me again, Oliver. But honest, now, you're only thirteen inches tall, and you have a brother that can make a noise like *that*?"

"Well," said Oliver. "He's my *big* brother!"

"Some big brother!" said Yogi. "How big *is* he, for

Pete's sake? He sounds like he's as big as one of those elephants you were talking about before!"

"Elephant? Big as an elephant?" snorted Oliver. "He'd pick up an elephant like you'd pick up a grass-hopper!"

"But *why* is he making that noise?" persisted Yogi.

"Why? Goodness only knows!" answered Oliver. "He's not very bright, for one thing. You know how I

introduced myself—the Jolly Green Midget? Well, of course, I'm not at all jolly. I'm cranky and irritable most of the time. But that big, dumb brother of mine—he's *really* jolly! He goes stomping up and down *his* valley all day long, hollering 'Ho! Ho! Ho!' And *that's* the noise you hear. It sounds like thunder because he's so big and his voice is so deep. And those waves in the lake—that's on account of the ground shak-

ing from all the stomping up and down!"

"Wow!" exclaimed Boo Boo. "He can make waves in a lake just walking around? That's *big*!"

"My brother," said Oliver, "was, the last time he was measured, ninety-one feet tall and weighed nine thousand, four hundred and twelve pounds and two ounces! He's probably put on some weight since then," he added gloomily.

Yogi looked at Oliver. "Then if you're the Jolly Green Midget, even though you're not really jolly," he said slowly, "that would make Mr. Ho Ho Ho over there the Jolly—"

"Exactly!" said Oliver. "My brother is the real, genuine, Jolly Green Gi—" He broke off, as a series of thunderous "Ho Ho Ho's" drowned out whatever he was going to say.

"Where's your brother's

valley? How big is it?" asked Yogi.

"Just over the next rise," answered Oliver. "It's sixteen miles long and twenty-one miles wide."

"Hey!" cried Boo Boo. "Now *that's* what I'd call a *real* valley! Does he grow anything there?"

"Just about what I grow here," Oliver replied. "Corn and tomatoes and peas. Enough for himself, that's

all. His are a little bigger than mine, though!"

"I'll just bet they are!" laughed Yogi. "How big, Oliver?"

"Well," answered the little green man, "one of his ears of corn is the size of a really big motor boat. You couldn't get one of his tomatoes inside of a house, they're so big. And just *one* of his peas is as big as four or five basketballs!"

"I'll tell you something," said Yogi. "In spite of the fact

that you yell a lot and snarl at everybody, I think you're a nice guy, Oliver. But I wouldn't live around here if you paid me to!"

"You're just like everyone else!" snapped Oliver. "You just don't like green people!"

"What you just said is *not* one of the reasons I don't want to live around here," said Yogi slowly. "What difference does it make if you're green? People or animals aren't green or brown or big

or small—they're people or animals. It's what kind of people or animals—green or small has nothing to do with it!" He stopped for a moment and then went on, "The real reason we're gonna get away from here is that your brother makes so doggone much noise being jolly, I just can't stand it!"

"If you think it's noisy now, come back in a month!" said Oliver.

"What happens in a

month? Is big brother going to learn to play the drums?" said Yogi.

"That would be something, wouldn't it?" said Oliver. And for the first time, Yogi and Boo Boo heard him laugh. It came out as a sort of tinny "he he he." "I'd like to see those drums!" He stopped and did his "he he he" laugh again. "No," he went on. "Next month the rest of my family's coming!"

"Family? What family?" gasped Yogi.

"Oh, I have eleven brothers and five sisters," answered Oliver. "Then there are twenty or thirty uncles and aunts, and I guess maybe a hundred or so cousins!"

"I'm afraid to ask the next question," said Yogi. "Are they all as big as *he* is?"

"One of my sisters is just a teeny bit smaller," answered Oliver. "The rest of the family is bigger!"

Yogi just sat still for a moment. He was starting to get an idea which scared him half-to-death. Then he said, "That valley of your brother's—it's going to be a little crowded over there, isn't it?"

"Oh, they won't live in his valley," replied Oliver. "They're going to spread out all around here!"

"But, my goodness, Oliver," exclaimed Boo Boo,

"there aren't enough valleys to go around!"

"That's no problem for them," said Oliver. "They'll fix things to suit themselves!"

"How?" asked Yogi fearfully.

"They'll just tear down all the mountains," said Oliver. "Then they'll take all they've torn down, throw it all down hill until everything's level, and then each one of them will stomp out his own

valley! They'll have to move some rivers around, but that's no problem for *them*!"

"This is all going to happen in a month?" asked Yogi.

"Not quite," answered Oliver Irk. "They'll *be* here in a month. It may take them another week or two to decide *who's* going to live *where*. Then maybe another month before they get things all fixed up! Two months from now you won't know this place!"

"Where are they all coming *from*? And how do they keep in touch with one another?" Yogi wanted to know.

"I have absolutely no idea," said Oliver. "I haven't seen any of them—except *him*—for ages! And I really mean ages! They have some way of getting word around, but I don't know that, either. They never tell me anything. I think they're ashamed of me because I'm so little!"

Yogi looked at Boo Boo,

then at Oliver. He said, "Oliver, excuse us for a while. Boo Boo and I have some talking to do!"

"Sure," said the tiny green man. "See you later. I've got some corn to hoe, anyhow. Oh, quiet!" he screeched, as another "HO HO HO" thundered through the mountains.

The two bears returned to where they had slept the night before. Yogi said to Boo

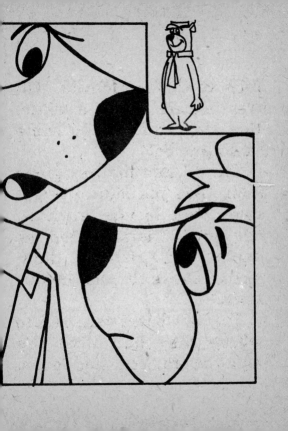

Boo, "You know what this means, don't you, chum?"

"I think so," said Boo Boo. "This'll wreck Jellystone!"

"Then there's only one thing we can do, isn't there?" went on Yogi. "We've got to tell the Ranger about this!"

"But he'll *cage* us!" wailed Boo Boo:

"I don't think so," Yogi replied. "I think this might be just what we're looking for— a way to get the Ranger to forget what we did! What *I*

218

did, I mean!" he added hastily. "If we can help him figure out a way to stop these jolly green characters, I think he'll *welcome* us back!"

"Well, all right, if you say so," said Boo Boo. "I'd sure hate to see them bust up the Park. I'd like to live here a long, long time!"

"Me, too!" replied Yogi. "Let's go, then! We haven't got too much time left!"

"There's just one thing, though," said Boo Boo.

"What's that?" said Yogi.

Boo Boo looked at him. "You think he'll believe us? Green midgets? Giants? Tearing down mountains?"

"Oh-oh!" said Yogi. "I never even thought of *that!*" He paused and thought for a little while. "Well," he said, "I don't like to do it, but there's only one thing we *can* do!"

"What's that?" said the little bear.

"Take Oliver Irk along

with us and *show* him to the Ranger!" snapped Yogi. "He'll *have* to believe it, *then*!"

"Gosh, Yogi!" said Boo Boo. "You think he'll be willing? It's his family that wants to move in!"

"I don't care if he's willing or not—he's going!" said Yogi. "If I have to, I'll just pick him up and take him along!" And that's what they did. For the first couple of hours, Yogi just carried

Oliver Irk in one hand. But
the tiny green man made so
much noise, screeching and
screaming, that Yogi finally
sat Oliver on his shoulder
and told him to hang on and
shut up! It didn't take Oliver
long to realize that if he fell
off Yogi's shoulder, he'd
break a leg or an arm or
some ribs or maybe even his
neck.

The trip back took only
three days because it was all
downhill. When they ap-

proached the Ranger's cabin, he was nowhere in sight. "He's inside at his desk," said Yogi. "Boo Boo, keep a tight hold on Oliver. I'm going in without him!"

When Yogi entered the cabin, the Ranger looked up and almost fell out of his chair. Then he looked Yogi up and down and said, "I suppose I'd better listen to what you have to say to me. It had better be awful good, because if it isn't, you'll be in

a cage in fifteen minutes!"

Yogi walked in, sat down, and told Ranger Smith the whole story. When he finished, the Ranger said, "It's pretty good, Yogi, but not quite good enough." He reached for the phone.

"Don't use the phone yet, Ranger Smith," Yogi said. "I haven't finished yet! Boo Boo! Bring him in!"

When Boo Boo came through the door with Oliver, the Ranger *did* fall out of his

chair! His eyes bulged out and got as big as saucers! Then he looked at Boo Boo, Oliver, and finally at Yogi.

"It's true, then?" he said. "This is the Jolly Green Midget? And all that other stuff? The mountains and all that?"

"Every word," said Yogi. "And we've got to stop it, somehow!"

This time when Ranger Smith reached for the phone, Yogi didn't try to stop him.

One hour later, after a long series of calls, the Ranger turned to Yogi and said, "I've talked to everybody. They're all running around in circles, because short of an atomic bomb, how can we stop this thing?"

Yogi had been sitting in a corner, staring out of the window. Without turning around, he said, "Ranger Smith, I just remembered something Oliver said about those mountains giving off

smoke a long time ago. These mountains are part of the Rockies, aren't they?"

"They're the Rockies, all right," answered the Ranger. "They're part of a chain that goes from Alaska all the way down into South America. What's that got to do with anything?"

"Well, if they used to give off smoke, then they used to be volcanoes. Right?" said Yogi. Without waiting for an answer, he went on. "What

do you suppose will happen if these green giants start tearing them down? Won't that start them up again?"

The Ranger just stared at Yogi. "Of course!" he yelled, as he jumped for the phone and made a call. He was on the phone for quite a while. Finally he finished and spoke directly to Oliver Irk.

"Mr. Irk," he said, "I have a message for your family. I don't know how big they are. I've never met them. From

what Yogi says, I guess they *could* tear down some of these mountains to make room for themselves. But if they open up volcanoes, they're liable to start this whole chain into eruption! They may not care what happens to anybody else, but when volcanoes start to let go, *nothing* is big enough or strong enough to come out alive! That is the message. You skedaddle back up there, and tell your brother to get

word to the family to stay where they are. If they try to move into Jellystone and tear it up the way they plan, they'll all be dead! Yogi, you and Boo Boo go with him and make sure he delivers the message! When you get back, I want to see you!"

"You mean we can *come* back?" yelled Yogi.

"Well," said the Ranger. "You *saved* the Park. I guess the least I can do is let you *live* in it!"